A Poetic Poop.

Denzil Dias

Published by Denzil Dias, 2024.

Also by Denzil Dias

Short Life, Shorter Stories Series
NIL - Nilofer

Standalone
A Poetic Poop.

Table of Contents

A POETIC POOP: _COLLECTION OF POETRY NOT MEANT TO BE_

Poetry is like pooping _If there is a poem inside you, it has to come out Sometimes it can be really difficult and take longer than you'd like (it may even be painful), but other times it can be really easy and happen much faster than you expected but either way – it is important, and it feels so much better when it's done –_ **Quote by Sarak Kay**

POEM 1: BE CURIOUS TO VOLUNTEERING

Curiosity never killed any cat
Never let any ill – willed phrase
kill your curiosity even before you start to bat
Be curious to new things
Be curious to new places and peoples
Be curious to new happenings
Be curious to Volunteering
Every tree in off season sheds its leaves
Humans too need to shed our veneers
And see for ourselves what wood we are made from?
At Sadhana Forest
It's not about "Coming"
It's about "Welcoming"
Self and Others
At Sadhana Forest
It's not labour, it's Love for life
It's not work, its Seva or Service
The forest has given us fruits, flowers, fish, fragrances, and Oxygen so
fresh to one and all
Even to those humans who did not work, contribute or donate
anything to the forest at all
The forest asks you to visit as a guest,
Volunteer as the rest
Live, Laugh, Learn, and Love

By putting yourself to the test
Be curious to new experiences Be curious to volunteer at Sadhana
Forest

POEM 2: WAITED FOR HER

Everyone at Sadhana Forest told me that she is extremely beautiful
She was a delight to the Sight as Salve to the Eyes
On a dark dreary night, she walked past my toilet light As I attended
to nature's call,
All I could see was her two tiny feet, So tender so Sweet
As I hurriedly reached for the Toilet water pail, she disappeared into
the misty morning trail
I decided to woo her, with my attractive charms I chose to invite her to
my private forest hut
I cleaned it, cleared the clutter, and cooked her delicious meals,
dressed the hut in colourful curtains
I patiently watched and waited with abated breath
Late past midnight she came She totally ignored me
She was too beautiful for me She was an act of creation She was
beautiful poetry in motion
And then in the blurry moonlit sky, she exposed and showed me her
naked beauty
In the dead darkness of the Sadhana Forest night, this Peahen mistook
me for a Peacock and opened its feathers and wings to attract me
Felt enthralled in enjoying the exhilarating beauty of this mesmerizing
peahen
**Come to Sadhana Forests where beautiful Peahens are waiting for
you**

POEM 3: DANCE HEALS

LIFE KILLS
Life is beautiful and sublime
Yet it ends with the passage of time
LUST LASTS
Lust is passion and not a crime
A must for life to be on the incline
LOVE HURTS
Love is the only drug that parents allow a child to get high on
The highs are heavenly and like having a ball
The lows are like climbing a wall
DEATH FREES
We are just tourists on planet earth
Death ends sadness & happiness
Connecting us to the cradle of birth
DANCE HEALS
Dance is medicine for the body
Magic for the mind
And music for the soul
Dance unites a man and woman
Making couples, complete & whole
Dance Heals It is divine

POEM 4: A "TUBIE" THAT'S WHAT I AM

Tall as a Tube light
But not as shining or bright
At Social functions, always standing in a Cool & Dark Corner
Waiting for some soul to notice me, once its dark enough
Off or on, I am always so white, maybe that's why they call me, "Cool
light"
Fit & Fine, I may be, fool me not, cool is not what I am from any sight
I am the Tube light and my Wife is the modern LED yellow florescent
light
In Cinema halls you will always find us,
the tube lighting your steps in the dark and the LED yellow lights
glowing high above and all around you, like fireflies in the night
It takes me a lot of blinks and flickers to finally get, TURNED ON
My Wifey the LED Bulb is always such a warm & bright soul, ever
ready and gets instantly TURNED ON
My brain is slow and my heart is steadfast
When jokes are cracked, I am the one to laugh the last
I miss one liners and witty remarks because my brain does not, fast,
light up
**As I concentrate in spreading cool white light all around, before
one can say what's up?**

POEM 6: A FACTUAL CHRIST'S BIRTHDAY

A simple birth event 2000 + years long, long ago
Divided history into BC and AD that is before and after Christ for
time to flow
Christ's birth introduced a new Gregorian calendar
For us to count our days till his second coming and to be pure & as
white as snow

Christ was not born on Christmas Day
For 2 Centuries after he was born, some human council decided to
celebrate Christ's birthday on 25th December the pagan Saturnalia
Sun festival way
The birth of the Pagan Sun was converted and made as the birth day of
God's only Son

Just as Adam was directly made by Almighty God
The second Adam, Jesus too was directly conceived by God Yahweh -
the self-existent one – the I AM that I AM
Jesus is not Jesus's name His original Hebrew birth name is
Yahushua, meaning Yahweh is my Salvation

Jesus was born in a village inn's barn
Just like any other Bethlehem cattle or animal farm
The skies were so blue, and a new Star shining so far

Winter not arrived, no snow falling, the Shepherds grazing their sheep
out in the open fields

Ancient Astrologers earlier known as Chaldeans
Part of the Evil King Herod's circle of so called "Wise Men"
Bible refers to them as, "Magi", today's short form for magicians

In Hebrew language they were "diviners", "divining the skies"
A practice condemned by the same God who created the earth and the
heavens

When the so called "wise men" met Jesus
He was no longer in a cattle barn,
But was grown young child and living in a house
As mentioned in Mathew: 2: 10, 11

Just like in the Garden of Eden God mentioned the forbidden fruit
But he did not mention if it was banana, mango, or apple to boot
Similarly, God mentioned only "Magi's" visiting Jesus, not 1 or 2 or 3
Wise men

Gold, frankincense, and Myrrh were gifts offered
Gold a symbol of kingship of the future king of kings
Frankincense incense of sweet fragrance
Myrrh an embalming oil, a symbol of death

Jesus was born a Jew and Joseph and Mary were Jews too
They never celebrated Jesus's birthday
As it was not an Eastern culture to honour
The day of your birth in any celebratory way
Till the age of becoming a 30 years old gentleman

Jesus was always known as the humble carpenter's spawn (Son)

Not a single year did Jesus celebrate and glorify his own day of birth
on earth
Not a single scripture or commandment to celebrate his birth day after
his death

In the biblical day of Christ's birth on earth's terrain
There were no Xmas trees, no Snow falling,
No Santa Claus and his magical sleigh train

Christ is no longer a child to be born every year, again and again
He is long risen and gone to heaven
Waiting to come again as king of kings & ruler sovereign
What will he say, when he sees Christmas commercial activities done
in his name?

Christ's birth on earth was a blessing divine
But that does not mean we should drink in his name, rum and wine
Now with this factual Christ's Birthday Poem
In today's Xmas Celebrations
I leave you guessing, much less
What's factual and what's a fictional mess

POEM 7: EVERY DAY IS "WOMAN'S" DAY

She is Powerful

It takes 1 Breast feeding Woman as a mother approximately 20 years to make the Boy Child into a Man

It takes just 20 days for another woman to jiggle her breasts and make that same Man into a Child in her warm loving embrace

She adds Value

Men seek for their mother in the wife; they cherish and laugh

They admit, female partners are their better half

Women in many respects complete Men

Yet never heard a Woman referring to her man as, "He is my bitter or better half"

She aids in Construction & Destruction too

Behind every successful man is 1 woman

Behind every destroyed man, there are 2 women

One makes a man's life wonderful; one becomes WOE to the MAN

A deadly woman

Women can be Gender Neutral & free

Woman can become "Manly", but man is not allowed to explore his feminity

So many dresses and garments and still Woman can jump into "Men's Pants"

A man cannot dare to wear a female's dress, lest he is a "Cross Dresser" or Gay & even if he's got ants in his pants

Ruling the Roost

Woman can become House Wives and title themselves as House Manager's too

The same woman can get out of the house and earn her bread and butter & cheese as well

Man cannot do the same, if he is a house husband, he cannot swell in pride or yell & tell

Women are Heroine's as well as Heroes in real life

Only Brave & Courage's females can be referred to as "Hero"

Imagine men being given the title of doing something good for humankind as "Heroine"

Women work harder than men

Women can compete in every field and sphere of life

When large groups of men are working together, they put up a sign, "Men at Work"

Men after daily work can just sit and ask, but the woman after a job too, does at home multitask

Women are Vessels of God's great creation

Man's Chromosomes decides, if it is a baby boy or baby girl, but the woman's womb says, "No Questions Asked"

Women can make a man's every day look like a "Honeymoon" or he can be made lost to go to the moon

Here is my Compliment to all Good & Kind-hearted Women

In my REBIRTH or RESURRECTION to God, I would Plead & Request if I may walk on earth ever again, may I be born as a woman to give others Pleasure or Pain

POEM 8: INTERNATIONAL DANCE DAY PLEDGE

Dance alone or dance along in a group
But dance like Chicken in a Coup
Damn those who watch and hoot
Pity they cannot dance; they can hear the chicken (music) but not
smell the soup

Sing alone in the Shower or sing along with the group
Sing as if no one is listening to your cry & cough
Damn those who look and laugh
Be happy that Music moves our bodies & our soul

Love always again and again
Even knowing that at the end there is just hurt and pain
Pretend that you have never been in love and never been hurt
Live another day by dancing and romancing on Planet Earth

Love needs two partners always
The sound of music and dancing feet
Until they meet, music and dance are not so sweet

POEM 9: LAID ON THE BED, BUT DID NOT GET LAID

On milky white bed sheet spread
Hot summer days & hotter body of yours in bed
Your smooth & silky legs nicely spread eagled and widespread
You were the butter and I was the bread

We just laid and chatted to our hearts content
Even though I was aroused and had a different intent
The Cool AC breeze blowing on one hot body & one hot mind
I will surely go back in time, to unwind & rewind

And then we kissed and closed our eyes
I could not taste the chocolate with our lips so entwined
It was pure bliss and heavenly divine
I did not even feel the need of Urak (local Goan brew) or Wine

Listening to you speak is a sweet sensation
Mentally I am undressing you slowly in slow motion
And we just laid there on bed with so less action
And absolutely no Penetration

You were waxed with your pussy prepared
I got my family jewellery cleaned and Anne Frenched
You did not loosen yourself out

Neither did I force myself in

Just being in your semi naked presence, gave me a high
And the ceiling walls were not four but five
Hours have gone by, but your words, they still linger,
Wanting my fingers to feel your breasts so young & tender
My Balls were so full
My Missile ready to strike
But it was just gonna be first base today
Looking forward to Second & Third base someday

POEM 10: WHAT'S UP? MY DANCING DOLL

Opened my what's app, late at night, after wearing my sleeping
upholstery
Saw a beautiful damsel, frozen in prose and poetry

As a child had a dancing doll toy that stood on its two fixed feet,
standing cute & tall
Made of mud and clay it stood silently still till my touch breathed life
into it, making it sway

Now am, a grown-up man
On my what's app, a video waits for my fingers touch to put on and
play
This dancing dolls video, if I may
This new dancing girl is here to stay

Cause she twists and turns and twirls her dress away
Dressed in black pleated skirt
She is so full of cheer and mirth

My dancing doll toy was made from mud, clay, and earth
This dancing doll is made from flesh, blood & bones right from birth

Seeing my dancing doll come alive
My mind is wide awake
In sleeping mode, I gave my dancing doll
A standing ovation to my live dancing doll

POEM 11: MY IMAGINARY MIND

Oh no! The Travels & Travails
Of my Imaginary Mind
Oh, how it can be so unkind
Mind your own business
Says my very own Mind

Man, yet cannot travel in past in time
But the same mind can travel to the future so sublime
High on hills of Nandidurg,
More monkeys and couples in pairs than in Coorg

Perched like an Eagle roaring to soar
I reach out to touch the clouds, so just below
I almost touch them and & they are almost not there
The blazing Sun above me, the Soothing Clouds below me
If this is Paradise, if this is Paradise, let it be

Once upon a time, as a child, i was encouraged
To have an imaginary friend
Today here i am a fully grown-up man
Standing on Nandi Hills with an Imaginary Cyber Friend

Discussing & debating with her
What is a Mountain and what is a Hill?

Wondering how long it takes a Mole to become a hill?
Nandi hill clouds make the rain
And here i am riding my bike and crying again
Nandi hills teach a lot
Rains becomes rivers, lakes come from melted snow
Tiny little seeds into gigantic Oak trees they grow
The azure blue Sky is glorious in its blueness
The white Cotton Clouds are there to caress
Oh how i wish, it was you besides me
And not this imaginary friend

Travelling back home
Leaving found memories of mesmerizing occasions
Spend with an imaginary companion
Leaving Nandi hills, I make a wish
At Bhoga Nandeeshwara Temple
"Lord Shiva, the next time I travel in real time
May my Cyber Friend be walking with me
On Nandi hills, hand in hand"

POEM 12: YOUR BOOBS MAKE ME WANT TO BECOME A BABY AGAIN

Your picture of two big boobs, so firm & so bursting full of milk and
blood
Just staring at them, makes me feel like a Stud
So soft tissue to the eyes
Like 2 Big Juicy Burgers or Pies

Wheatish Colour, like the best of brown wheat just harvested in
Want to dip my fingers, hands and my mouth too in your breasts skin
38 C it is that's what you say
Bless them, Lord I pray, may they grow day by day
Oh the journey, to be between your two mounts (Mountains)
Want to rest my tired soul, between the cushion of your too soft
melons
Hands I have so few, to hold such a lot of boo boos (boobs)
Holding them would feel as, one hand in Earth and one in heaven
Open your breasts wide for me
Luv to hold your Big Boobs, while you hold my Small Balls
Will rest my lips and lick your nipples
Where I could see no hair follicles
Looking at your Big Bursting Boobs
I want to become a Baby once again
To suckle and bite
And scream in delight

POEM 13: NEVER KNEW A GOOD TEACHER

School days were more of fear than educational fun
Used to walk to school and it was always a homeward run
School was best closed on holidays, for us to play and roam
Never knew of a Good Teacher, pleasant memories of none

For teachers, it was just another profession
For student's attendance at school, just another necessary compulsion
Swollen knuckles and swollen feet
Are all what stupid students get for not being the teacher's sweet

School days were more of fear than educational fun
Used to walk to school and it was always a homeward run
School was best closed on holidays, for us to play and roam
Never knew of a Good Teacher, pleasant memories of none

When we were commanded to voluntarily join RSP (Road Safety
Patrol)
Denzil's creativity called it RSP (Road Side Pigs),
They tempted us to join with free snacks every day
On doing our road side service we would get Ragda, Samosa & Pattice
the RSP way

School days were more of fear than educational fun

Used to walk to school and it was always a homeward run
School was best closed on holidays, for us to play and roam
Never knew of a Good Teacher, pleasant memories of none

English class and it was Deepak's turn, to "make a sentence with two words" and learn
Mrs Fizardo gave Denzil two big words, Discovery, and Invention
I created a sentence with pure of heart and clean intention
What I got was "One Tight Slap" for my creation

School days were more of fear than educational fun
Used to walk to school and it was always a homeward run
School was best closed on holidays, for us to play and roam
Never knew of a Good Teacher, pleasant memories of none

My created sentence was: My Father DISVOVERED my Mother and INVENTED me
Never knew of a Good Teacher Thought of teaching the teacher a good lesson
Someday hope life teaches her a good session

School days were more of fear than educational fun
Used to walk to school and it was always a homeward run
School was best closed on holidays, for us to play and roam
Never knew of a Good Teacher, pleasant memories of none

Life was the greatest & best teacher
All around you there were so many samples and examples
For information, knowledge, and intelligence we need to be ever seekers

School days were more of fear than educational fun
Used to walk to school and it was always a homeward run
School was best closed on holidays, for us to play and roam
Never knew of a Good Teacher, pleasant memories of none

Every day we live can be a certificate course
Every week we survive can be a diploma awarded
Every month we learn to earn can be a graduated progress
Every year we celebrate our birthday with grateful love can be a PHD rewarded

POEM 14: SIMPLY

Your Pretty face
A face a simple as simple can be
A smile as special as special can be
Your face, your face, your face
Will not stop staring, even if hit with a mace

Your full-blooded lips
Your lips as lips can ever be
So full of blood and fulfilling
So Curvaceous and thrilling
A kiss on your pouting lips would be so chilling

Your Soul-Searching eyes
Your Lotus like dark eyes
Are like Lilies in a clear blue pond
Which i know i will grow of very fond
So true is your name too
Simply ___________________

Your Dumpling Nose
A perfect shaped nose
Sandwiched between 2 chubby cheeks
Your cheeks are so full of blood
Waiting to be caressed and cuddled

Your Sexy Hair
Most of all special is your long lovely hair
That caresses and covers all your assets so much with care

If long as your knee it would be
Then there would be no better dress
To cover up in hair your wonderful and curvaceous body

POEM 15: SONG OF THE SARONG

An adjustable garment, so is the Sarong
Embraces all body types, the thin, the weak & the not so strong
A charming piece of cloth, adorned accurately it's a beach wear
Dress it like the Hippies, & it displays your assets, here & there

The Sarong can see! The sarong can hear
It can have a crush on the body it holds so near & dear
Your soft & soothing words flow & fall slowly on my head
Like the crushing of a soft feather bed

From the deep recesses of my mind
Something's to see, something's to share,
Before i am folded & put somewhere behind
Crushing against your body, having a crush on you, but from behind

Sometimes you wrap me round and round and all around
Against your warm body so sexy and sound
I love it when nothing comes between me and your two beautiful
mounds

Sometimes, this Sarong sees you in shorts
Sometimes in your Bra n Bikini, that's when it just gets too hots
The silent sarong sees it all
The best i like when you are undressed, standing naked, yet tall

This Sarong has no shadow of doubt
You are most beautiful, all of south & all of north
My heart Sighs & Sings, to your tune
Every time i see you, morning, night and at noon

This Sarong likes all of you
Your mischievous eyes
Your full-blooded luscious lips
Your chubby cheeks
Your wholesome and fulsome breasts
Your, on the rocks, rocking butts
Your white chocolate like smooth skin
Your long legs, a ladder to heaven
Your two tiny feet that holds all of the above

This sarong sees within you an angel by daylight
And a devil within the darkness of the deep night
I see you as a princess of the day & a Queen of delight

This sarong has wrapped many beautiful damsels, some small, some
tall
But you are the cutest of them all
Between your two valleys, my fabrics pass
Heaven is above & below is Earth
Your two warm breasts are to me, Hearth
And your birth place for me to comfortably berth

This Sarong says that_______________________ (name of your choice),
You have it all
The Cake, the Cream, the Cherry on top of it, standing tall
A rare Blend of Beauty and Brains
Add to it a beautiful heart, soothing soul, and intelligent mind

POEM 16: WET RAIN ON MY BODY

Rain drops, why you keep on falling
Can't you see my beautiful maiden has forgotten her umbrella today

My Desires for her are so hot that your raindrops will bounce away
My Wishes cannot be washed away by your incessant rains, not alteast
today
Who needs an Umbrella to stay dry, when i have such a beautiful
damsel walking my way

Flaming desires on my mind, why are you making me so wet oh
unkind rain
Roses may be red and Violets may be blue
To me Oh My _________________, you are my blossoming Rain
flower too

Mind is full of your love desiring you in pain
Body is soaked wet from this falling rain
My desire for you cannot get drained
Rains come again next time, & will have my _________________in
open arms again

Attraction is such a lovely feeling
There is no limit to our dreams, our desires, no sky, no ceiling

You make me feel so light; i think i could fly
Let's enjoy these moments of passion & desire, you are sexy and i will
be sly

These dark black rain clouds will someday go away
But you my love are meant to stay forever in my embrace, every day
Raindrops falling so softly, sticking like petals on her beautiful body
like sweet molten clay

Even the dew drops from heaven want to wet & touch my maiden's
body, **so pure like a temple's idol that is bathed in milk every day**

POEM 17: THANK GOD FOR COMPETITION

Competitors are better than friends
They do better for me than my friends

Competitors laugh at my errors and make sure that I don't ever repeat
them
Friends tend to overlook them

Friends are too polite to point out my weaknesses, but my competitors
advertise them
Thus, make me change

I have no complaints against competitors who charge less, give less and
make a mess

Competitors are a blessing in disguise
Where there are more competitors, there is always more business

Competitors don't mind their own business
They pay more attention to my business & help me to manage it better

I do Thank God for such Competition
I do not worry about competing

Because even the Gods, do have competition

POEM 18: SOON COMING MONSOON

Oh! How momentarily the monsoon comes and goes,
Wish it could stay longer, to wet my toes,
Can cry in public only in the rain,
Wet my pains and let it drizzle down the drain,
Oh! Rains please do come soon again

Can wear old clothes again,
No need to be fashionable in the rain,
Need not iron my clothes neat and dry,
Thanks to the monsoons, even my clothes can cry

Oh! How momentarily the monsoon comes and goes,
Wish it could stay longer, to wet my toes,
Can cry in public only in the rain,
Wet my pains and let it drizzle down the drain,
Oh! Rains please do come soon again

Everything once again is so clean and green,
Thanks to the rains, it keeps nature so clean,
The sky is the shower and the world the restroom,
Everything is so wet and so fresh and in bloom

Oh! How momentarily the monsoon comes and goes,

Wish it could stay longer, to wet my toes,
Can cry in public only in the rain,
Wet my pains and let it drizzle down the drain,
Oh! Rains please do come soon again

Oh! The first smell of falling rain,
Who has not experienced is not living again,
Oh! The pit a patter sound of the incessant rain,
Who has not enjoyed the sound of nature's music so sublime
Oh! Rains please do come soon again

POEM 19: A LADY CALLED LYDIA

As a teenager while growing up in Mumbai
Shy as a young boy, but knew of hot neighbour living nearby

Knew of a neighbour who was known as wife of Santan
Her skin was perfectly white and never knew, what is a Suntan

Lydia is a feminine first name of Greek origin meaning, "beautiful one"
Lucky few, they have matching names to their matching "beauty two"

I asked here where is she from? Mangalorean or Anglo Indian?
Her Turkish name confused me all the same There is even a "Lydian" language to her name

The Bible describes an ancient Lady Lydia at Acts 16:14, 15 written here in poetic brief:

Lady called Lydia from the city of Thyatira
A dealer in luxurious purple cloth most expensive in the full of Phillipia
Worshipper of the good LORD Yahweh
With an open and responsive heart to Paul's WORD
She and her full family were baptized
A believer in Yeshua

She invited Paul to stay at her house, which was priceless

As a growing up teenager, I felt in Lydia, there was some magical lustre
Her beauty could make any man feel high like on dope (drugs)
She was the Apostle Paul's first transfigure (convert)
And thus, the first convert to Christianity in Europe

She says that she has a sweet tooth
Also, that she is not a good cook
Sweet deserts and baked stuff are what she likes
She has three adorable children that make her life, a delight

POEM 20: A LADY CALLED "DANUTA"

Born with a name that is truly Hebrew
Always in her hand is a Malt or Wheat hops beer brew

Having a feeble body and her mind keeps not many a grudge
She is true to her name: Danuta means, "God is Judge"

This Danuta, I know is born in France
But to me, in Goa, she is always in a Trance

Her name, Danuta reminds me of the songs, "Touch my heart" chorus
Of famous singer Danuta Lato of yesteryear, way back in 1986

She lives with her family with many bonds so strong
Does not want any, "man" to bring out in her all the wrongs

Always seen her in Tees, Quarts & Shorts
And she sells stuff from the Army that she Imports

Danuta is a woman that walks the talk and bites the bark
A flame full of love, which is waiting for the right spark
She is Daddy's child and Mama's pet
Waiting for a perfect lover, if such species exist, I dare to bet

She loves to jabber
Sometimes her words are as sweet as sugar
And sometimes as sharp as a dagger

In few words and no more
Hope this poem does not force me, to run to Lahore
Danuta Be yourself You are Strong, Sexy and a Beautiful Videshi
(foreigner)
**(For Indians the Hindi language word is "Desi" For foreigners it is,
"Videshi")**

POEM 21: COLOURS OF LIFE

Swaddled in cleanest clean whites, i arrive
Wondering why everyone is smiling, while i am crying

In white's i am welcomed
In white's i will be departed

Naked i come, they say
But naked they won't let me go away

If whites for purity, what's for me?
If reds for compassion, what's for me?
If blacks for mourning, what's for me?

Colours of life are seen everywhere
i wonder what's the colour of "humanity", is it seen anywhere?
What's the colour of humanity, by the way?

POEM 22: THE LADY IN RED

There she was perpendicular under the parapet of the building
Knowing that her fold-able umbrella was well tucked in her hand
purse
Yet she was letting out both, under her breath, wishes and curses
Hoping that he will offer her shelter under his large red umbrella from
the rain so unyielding
The rains so heavy and unmerciful the damsel so wet and looking so
pitiful

Oh my God, give this boy some courage, to help this dame in distress
He manages to gather his guts, and approach the girl He stutters and
stammers and finally answers

Excuse me Miss, "Is this the way to the Library Section" "No, it's the
opposite building, past the little garden "He thanks her and turns
around to go on away
This damsel loves to make her own wishes & her own way She mutters
under her wet breath; "I am waiting for this rain to stop, so that I too
can go to the same library, have some books to take away"

"Come join me, under my umbrella, if you don't mind staying little
wet and little dry", says the boy The wet & weary eyed damsel replies,
"As long as my books don't get wet" But books you do not have any
says the perplexed boy The girl replies, 'I will have many, on my way
back to the hostel where I stay"

There appeared a "Twinkle" in the eye of the beholder boy as he understood that this rainy day was his lucky day. **All it took was an Umbrella to make the way**

POEM 24: THE LADY IN RED

This young gal, always seen her dressed in flowery prints & petite
pinks
Always remember her well balanced whitish skin tone, between two
sisters, one little dark and the other like a Wheatish ice cream cone
Time flies, so do butterflies Budding little gal grows into a blossoming
flower so tall
This modest & meek looking girl, with parent's tender loving care,
grew to become a beautiful Goan pearl
Beautiful flower has so many stages of development, seen her at
"Peduncle" first and then directly at full "Petal" flowery growth
Today she stands proudly tall, Beauty, Brawn & Brains all bundled
into one voluptuous body & balls
I see her in Pics n Photos on what's app here & there
Here is what my wandering & roving mind has to share
This Lady in Red dress, standing on some palatial stairs
Makes my two eyeballs to continuously stare
Wide sparkling smile, like the shining sun
Sweet smiles, may the sun shine & warm thy heart
In this sweet spread, I have no part
This Lady in Red has no Palace of her own
Still to me she is like some Princess unknown
Robed in a blood red Skater dress, skin hugging and tight
Sleeveless & Short to my hearts delight
Sports shoes, on her demure feet, reflect her sporting character
Her original white skin, sun tanned like the desert's dusky sands

Saw another picture of her, Black dress with red stripes,
Followed the stripes path, wherever my eyes lured & led,
She is as beautiful as any fine satin bed spread
Her beauty is blissful and my crush is bashful
Pretty lips and plump hips
Where was I when God made this?
Her legs so full and slender
Reminds me of my favourite, "Chicken Leg Piece" so tender
First seen you as a child, when you were innocently just seven
Now your long beautiful legs are like a, "Ladder to Heaven"

This lady in Red is like the colour of blood & fire
Withholding within itself a raging passion and desire
Red is the colour of love and lust
Self-Survival & Self-Satisfaction is a must
Medical research has shown the power of Red in elevated blood
pressure, enhanced libido, increased respiratory rates, enhanced
metabolism, increased enthusiasm, higher levels of energy, and
increased confidence
The above qualities are in you, Oh Lady in Red!
Red is highly visible colour Able to focus attention quickly and get
people to make quick decisions, fire trucks and fire engines are usually
painted red Flashing red lights mean danger or emergency, while stop
signs and stop lights use the colour red to alert drivers
To me a Sensual & Shapely Lady in Red
Is like a Sexy Siren Shouting, "Let's jump into Bed"

POEM 25: WAITING FOR YOU

A boyfriend is a friend
A husband, a band like bond with no end
Boyfriend is always just a call away
Husband must be reminded to come on time everyday
Why is it always this way?
Why does a boyfriend change as a husband?
I have lost my boyfriend in never never land
Boyfriend understands your every need
Husband must be told, what to do, indeed
Boyfriend is like a perfumed hand written greeting card
Husband just another E - Male

Married my husband and lost my boyfriend
After marriage my boyfriend became husband
Can I unmarry? And find back my boyfriend once again?

POEM 26: SECRETS UNDER THE SKY

(Background of the poem is in a Military Cantonment Garden)
This Bold & Beautiful Damsel enters the room wearing her shortest
skirt;
She could ever wear
She parks her two cute big butts and occupies the Cushioned Chair
Gives my full body, Goosebumps and makes my hair stand,
everywhere
Her Short Skirt is not an invitation or instigation too
It's not an indication to other ladies, that I have beautiful legs two
Neither it's a provocation for the other kind and to make them woo
Her Short Skirt is to show that Chicken legs need not only be eaten
They can make Mighty Men so easily to be, "Smitten"
It's also about discovering, the beauty of the thighs
Gives so many men, without any drinks the highs
Tiny Chicken legs with full power lower calves
The Short Skirt shows a little and hides a lot of her femurs (Inner
thighs)
As she gets up and walks the Garden Stairs like a Ramp
Gives me a feeling of getting somewhere hot and somewhere damp
For some she is dressed to taunt, for others to flaunt
The Cool Monsoon breeze blows her Mini Skirt here and there
Her two feet are grounded Her breasts are full of abandonment
She is here Hot & Happening in this Military Cantonment
Her dress is her cheerfulness

Her devilish body her Artfulness
Her flirting dress, showing what's hot
And what's not your assets
Her short skirt is like a Teaser
Like my ever-favourite Strawberry breezer
To the Alpha males, she is Initiation, Excitation & Appreciation
This modern dressed girl is from the land of Kamasutra (Lovers
Scriptures)
Sleeveless dress, short skirt, High Heels, she makes me feel like a
Bhumiputra (Son of the earth)
Her body is pure poetry and passion
Her movements are like Yoga in action
So many Secrets under the dark Starry Sky
So many Surprises, under her Skirt flying so high
Just like the Shining Stars of the night
I get a brief glimpse of her black lace panties so tight
With this view, I say to her, Good Night

POEM 27: GOT A HEADACHE AND ENJOYED IT TOO

To visit Toastmaster's class, I mustered enough courage
Green tea and buttered toast were my evening food and beverage
Self-interested and self-invited myself as a guest
Was worried that I don't end up becoming a pest
The wooden benches took me back to school
Got to know, oh my God, in Toastmaster's there are so many rules
Born in a land of India, where we are taught, with folded hands to say,
Namaste, every day
Here I was seeing one and all, hand shaking, the Toastmaster's
International way
Expected the Toastmaster to offer us, like at Christian Weddings, here
in Goa (India) Cake and Wine
But what we got is fresh patties, crispy wafers, and cool drinking water
divine
Anyone was democratically voting for everyone
And everyone was happily evaluating anyone
Two hours of public talks
Were torture on body and mind
Thanks to Toastmasters
Who left at least, politicians and priests' false speeches behind
Got a Toastmaster's headache and enjoyed it too!
And listening to (or reading) this poem of mine, may you get a sweet
one too

POEM 28: ALL I HAVE SUCCUMBED TO IS LUST

Have not understood life itself;
Arrival, on Planet Earth, but not by my choice
Departure, from Planet Earth, too not much at our choice
Seeing people around trying to understand love for self;
All I have succumbed to is lust
All around I see, is people asking for Questions;
Living life, incomplete with, questions, self-answered
Probing for meaning, searching for solutions;
Doing the same things, that others are doing
Still the end is the same as the beginning
One man dared to ask questions; Gautama Buddha
But for every Question he answered More questions got created
Where does one come from? Where does one go? Does anyone know?
Life is like a Passenger Train, for some Third class, Second class or First class
All know that further down the Railway Bridge is broken, and in death do all of us part
But into that train, still we climb, clamber, and bring more to crawl into
This pursuit of understanding life, love, and lust
Has taken me, more than half of a lifetime, also for most
Life & living is a compulsion Has anyone stopped breathing & stopped living?

There is a hole to feed your stomach There is a hole to fill your lungs There is a hole to feed your mind but there is no hole to fill love in our heart

The Heart is & has always been a "Bloody Pump" The Mind is & has always been the "CPU" (Central Processing Unit") or Brain

Poets have long said that where there is life, there is love, where there is love, there is lust and where there is lust; there is life and this they say is the circle of life

This Poet has gone the other way round In lust can there be love found; in that love can the meaning of life be found?

All I have is succumbed to, is Lust I say again All I have succumbed is to Lust

POEM 29: AN OASIS IN THE DESERT OF MY MIND

Wake myself, wondering was I daydreaming? Soothe myself, to sleep
again
Slipping deep down in a dream, within a dream
I awaken myself on a desert plain
The scorching desert sun, not causing any pain
I thirst, not for Waters of life
I thirst for Springs of love, an quenchable thirst
This imaginary dessert offers Oasis of life supporting water
I ache for an oasis of love, to satisfy my soul
On the horizon, I see a shining silhouette in the sky
See her running in Bollywood style, slow motion towards me
Gliding gracefully like a white horse in the deserts golden sands
She seems well built and well-bred like an Arabian Horse of this land
A realist that I am Is the desert heat playing games with my mind?
I go along & add my imaginations to this mind game of mine
She paces her steps, so slowly & seductively,
that now I can see her more clearly
Her sweet desserts like body, draped in a white on black polka dot
dress
With every step she takes, a white polka dot drops and falls off her
dress
Golden Sands, white woman in black dress This is just an Oasis
Just see No Touch No caress
Polka dot dress I saw Could there be Polka dot lingerie too?

At the flick of my imaginary lashes,
I make the rich black dress disappear into the desert's ashes
No polka dots anymore Got to see rich black Lacy lingerie
And much more as the vision was approaching me, it was faintly
disappearing into the desert mist
Last of it, I could not miss Are 2 Conical pyramids, made for
heavenly Bliss Heaven is above and below is EARTH Your 2 warm
breasts to me are HEARTH And your Birth place for me to myself,
comfortably BERTH

POEM 31: TOUCHED BY A BUTTERFLY

A flower stands fixed in the soils of time
A butterfly has the freedom to fly around in different sands so sublime
Monarch butterflies are known to fly for more than 3000 miles
A blessed gift that some butterflies for millennia can easily navigate
Flowers are rooted to the soil and bounded within the farmer's estate
All flowers attract bats, birds, moths, beetles & bees to boot
But flowers are most happy when butterflies do their job too
Anthologists discovered that for cross pollination between flowers
They depend on animals, wind and the rain showers
Research in Floristry, has found and its incidental
When Bees, Butterflies, Moths, Flies & Birds pollinate plants, it's accidental
Flowers like & love it the most,
When colourful butterflies become their hosts
They carry their seed to the stigma to other flowers of their own species
All are doing what they were programmed to do, according to their own kind
If Butterflies had their very own mind, would they visit and sit on artificial flowers?
Made of Paper, Wood & Metal, yet artistic flowers to many of human kind
The real flowers that last only for a few days
Had lots to say to the Metal flower in the market of that day

The breeze blowing through your metal petals makes some noise we
can say
The molten brass shines in the daylight tricking butterflies that you
have nectar to share
Visiting butterflies help us "real flowers" to complete our plant life
cycle with care
Brass metal flower, made from earth, you are going to be burnt or
buried, some day
The Fat Golden Brass Metal Flower had nothing much to say
All it said was this," I felt lucky & blessed, to be touched by a beautiful
butterfly
**Nectars of life I did not have, All I had was, "Words" of
Conversation to share"**

POEM 32: THE SEXY SARI OR SAREE

Sari is an Indian dress, Devine by Design
Makes any woman to STAND OUT in any line
Drapes bodies of all SHAPES & SIZES
Girls, ladies, woman, it's for all ages

Sari neatly hand tucked on the waist, falls like a graceful waterfall
For all females one size fits all

Respectable is the Sari
So much you can show
And yet you cannot be degrading
It covers what I don't want and shows off what I want
The Saree's house is the BLOUSE
It tucks in my best assets, above
I can go Sleeveless, Braless, Neckless & Backless TOO
And none of the Traditionalists will BOO

6 yards or 9 YARDS
The Sari brings out the feminine beauty from every Indian
BACKYARD
Just one long sheet of material

Every sari is beautiful, even if left hanging on some shop wall

But when draped on a full-blown woman, makes her look more
elegant & taller

Sari is a body-hugging dress,
Wraps around all SHAPES and SIZES and CURVES
Sari is the only unstitched and untailored garment
Does not need, cutting, stitching or shaping

Indian woman adorns a sari OVER a Blouse (top) and Petticoat
(Ghaghara)
European woman loves to wear sari with nothing much UNDER
Makes most Indian men go ASUNDER (crazy)

Sari is my ever favourite
Takes longest to dress
And fastest to undress

Some wear Sari to appear BARING, DARING, OR CARING
To me every FAIR & LOVELY Woman looks in any Sari, ever more
ENDEARING

Saree's make me wonder
Does a Sari make a woman more desirable?
Or the lovely woman makes the Sari more beautiful?

Don't miss out!

Visit the website below and you can sign up to receive emails whenever Denzil Dias publishes a new book. There's no charge and no obligation.

https://books2read.com/r/B-A-MOWIC-ZJMXE

BOOKS 2 READ

Connecting independent readers to independent writers.

Also by Denzil Dias

Short Life, Shorter Stories Series
NIL - Nilofer

Standalone
A Poetic Poop.

About the Author

I am not a people pleaser. I am one diplomatic disaster about to happen. I speak my mind, break hearts (sometimes) and get myself hurt in the end. Just another simple tourist on planet earth.

I am a very deep person. So i like people who love stories, mysteries and enigmatic personalities. I love watching Bollywood and Hollywood movies, but the sensible ones only.

My hobbies are writing poetry and short stories, love debating, Black & White photography, discovering new waterfalls in the deep hinterlands all over India via Trekking or Hiking.

Love making new friends online. But only the sensible ones and i avoid the sentimental types so flooded in the Cyber world. I like people with some amount of "Emotional Intelligence".

I am a very humorous person. I consider myself as a "Tourist" on planet earth. I love to live this passage of life, laughing all the way.

Some may find me too deep, but then i cannot help if they do not know to swim in deep waters. he he Ignorance is surely a bliss i feel. Accurate knowledge or pure information is more of a pain.